LET'S G

Bicycle Man

Peter Simmonds

Scripture Union

© Peter Simmonds 1997
First published 1997

Scripture Union, 207–209 Queensway, Bletchley, Milton Keynes, MK2 2EB, England.

ISBN 1 85999 183 1

British Library Cataloguing-in-Publication Data.
A catalogue record of this book is available from the British Library.

Printed and bound in Great Britain by Cox and Wyman Ltd, Reading, Berkshire.

Contents

To my wife Kathy and our children
Stephen, Andrew, Philip and Ruth.

Chapter one

The end of the world

"Hey! Joel! Can't you go any faster?" Ben Green yelled as he sped past his brother.

"I'm going as fast as I can. I didn't want to race!" Joel slammed on his brakes and skidded to a halt by a tall pine tree as his brother disappeared over the brow of the hill.

"See you at home!" Ben's voice trailed into the distance. Joel stood with his bike resting between his legs. The wind blew the tops of the pine trees and made a noise like a faint whistle. Suddenly the forest became quiet. Joel could hear himself panting for breath. He wiped his brown hair away from his eyes as he stood wondering what to do next. He liked playing with Ben most of the time but today everything Ben did annoyed him.

Ever since Ben had got the new bike for his thirteenth birthday he had seemed a different person. All he wanted to do was play on bikes. Joel hadn't minded at first but he was getting a bit tired of it now. It wasn't as if there was anything wrong with Joel's bike. It just wasn't a mountain bike like Ben's and, well, it was second-hand too.

Joel pushed his bike up the hill and from the top looked down on the rest of Osterton Country Park, out across the tops of the trees to where he could see the small town of Edensbury three miles away. He free-wheeled down the forest track enjoying the wind in his face. At that moment he was completing the Olympic Mountain Biking time trial in record time. He stood up in the saddle, pedalling hard, weaving from side to side in a heroic bid for the line. Britain would be proud of its new gold medallist. Joel chested the imaginary tape and free-wheeled the remainder of the forest track with his arms aloft as the crowd cheered him loudly. He was jolted out of his dream as his front wheel hit a bump and the bike wobbled. Joel grabbed the handlebar and braked to a stop. His heart was beating very fast. Even great champions get scared it seems.

"Oh no! The shopping!" Joel groaned as he remembered Mum's request to get the bread and milk on the way home. That was probably why Ben had dashed off – just to get out of it. With a sigh, Joel mounted his bike again and set off in the direction of Edensbury.

The journey took only twenty minutes on the back road. As Joel cycled on the pavement down the busy High Street, he swerved to dodge the shoppers.

"Sorry, Mrs Murdoch!" The front wheel of Joel's bike caught the wheel of a woman's shopping bag, spilling its contents on the pavement. Joel stopped and helped the woman put the vegetables back in the basket.

"You slow down a bit, young Joel. This isn't a race track. You could hurt someone." Joel blushed as he leant his bike against the window of Albert's bike shop. The scruffy shop front looked out of place amongst the bright-fronted travel agent's, chemist's and greengrocer's shops. Joel loved looking in the window though. The shiny new mountain bikes were the best he had seen. Ben's bike hadn't come from there because Mum and Dad had said they were too expensive. The ones in here were much better than Ben's. Joel thought you could win an Olympic Mountain Biking medal on these bikes.

Reluctantly he tore himself away from Albert's shop and rode off in the opposite direction to Baines', the small supermarket on the corner of the High Street. He quickly leant his bike up against the drainpipe at the edge of the shop front, away from the trolleys. Checking his pocket for the money his mum had given him, he darted into the shop. He shivered as the cold air from the three fridges hit him. Moving round the store he caught the smell of the fresh bread from the bakery section. His tummy grumbled. Lunchtime.

He quickly picked up the loaves and two-litre

carton of milk and went to the checkout. Joel groaned as he saw the pile of shopping belonging to the tall, smartly-dressed elderly woman in front of him. This will take for ever, he thought.

As the woman carefully unloaded the trolley, Joel noticed her fingers. Four of them had rings on – gold with clusters of small glittering stones.

What a lot of rings, thought Joel. He noticed her silvery hair peeping out from under a green hat. Joel thought it looked a bit like an upturned flower pot. The pearls she wore round her neck were big and white. When she spoke she surprised Joel. "Young man, you may go first if you wish."

"Oh cool, thanks. You sure?" gasped Joel, but he was already pushing past to get level with the till.

Joel paid the checkout girl, put the milk and bread in one of Baines' green and white carrier bags and headed for the automatic door. The checkout girl called him back.

"Excuse me. You forgot your change."

"Oh yeah. Thanks." Joel grabbed the change and hurried from the store. He broke into a trot as he set off back down the High Street towards the alleyway between the chemist's and greengrocer's shop, which would take him onto the estate where he lived. He had only taken a few paces up the alleyway when he stopped.

"My bike!" One of the loaves rolled onto the ground as he dropped the bag. Joel didn't stop. He ran back into the glare of the spring sunshine in the

High Street. His eyes watered in the wind as he ran up the street. His chest began to hurt but he didn't stop running.

He arrived at the drainpipe where he'd left the bike. Joel's heart sank. No bike.

He ran backwards and forwards across the shop front, frantically trying to see if he had left it somewhere else. No bike.

He stopped. The lump in his throat threatened to rip a hole in his neck. "Where's my bike?" The mouse-like whisper went unnoticed except by the figure pushing her trolley across the path towards the car. It was the elderly woman with the rings.

"Is something wrong?" she asked.

"I can't find my bike. It's gone." Joel swallowed hard. He was staring in disbelief at the drainpipe. "It ... it's gone."

"Are you sure?"

"Yes, I left it here by this drainpipe and... it's gone!"

"Was it chained up?"

"No," came the weak reply. Joel began to cry.

"Well, let's see if the manager knows anything. With that, the elderly woman took Joel's arm and led him into the shop. Joel was in a bit of a daze as he wiped his cheek with the soft handkerchief she handed him.

"Why, Mrs Albert! What a nice surprise! Can I help you?" Joel noticed one of the manager's teeth was missing.

"I hope so, Mr Graham. This young man left his bike outside your shop whilst he did some shopping and now his bike has gone."

"Well, it's not the fault of Baines'. We make it perfectly clear..."

"Yes, yes, I know that, Mr Graham. I merely want to know if any of your staff saw anything."

"Yes, of course, Mrs Albert. What sort of bike are we talking about? "

Joel described his blue and yellow BMX as best he could. Mr Graham went to speak to his staff. This was all like a bad dream to Joel. What would his mum say? They could never afford another one. Ben had saved up for two years to help pay for his new bike.

Mr Graham strode down the aisle towards them. He was shaking his head. The woman patted Joel's shoulder as they walked back out of the shop. She was asking him where he lived so that she could take him home. Joel thanked her but said he could walk just as easily. His legs felt heavy as he plodded back to the alleyway, picked up the shopping and trudged home.

He felt as if this was the end of his world. How would he tell his mum and dad that he had lost his bike?

Chapter two

No bike!

Joel stood for a moment outside the back door. He caught his reflection in the glass panel of the door. His cheeks were streaked with tear stains. His mousy brown hair was ruffled and straggly from the battering the wind had given it. He had a look on his face that his mum would have described as "feeling sorry for himself".

His hand went for the door handle. He checked himself, wiped the sweat and dirt off his hand on the back of his trousers. Slowly he pulled the handle down and pushed the door open quietly with his shoulder.

Inside the kitchen, the smell of the left-over cooked lunch hit him. Joel could hear the muffled conversation from the dining room. Lunch was still going on. Joel didn't feel hungry any more and he felt as though he didn't want to see anyone just yet. He decided to try to sneak upstairs to his bedroom without being seen. Unfortunately, Digger, the family springer spaniel chose this moment to wake from his early afternoon sleep. On seeing Joel's back by the door into the hall, he gave a startled yelp and bounded from his basket under the kitchen table. As he did so, he caught the table leg, jolting the pie dish onto the floor with a smash. Joel turned in horror as the noise of the breaking pie dish echoed round the kitchen.

"Digger! What are you doing?" Mr Green's voice thundered from the dining room. The other door in the kitchen swung open and Mrs Green came in, still wearing her apron.

"Joel! When did you get in? Oh, look at this mess. Digger!" Joel could see into the dining room. His dad and Ben were sitting at the table. They were looking at him. Joel was wearing his favourite jumper with the red and white hoops. Ben said it made Joel look like a stick of rock because he was thin and the jumper was too big for him. This was rather unkind because Joel was a good-looking boy. He had a ready smile and a mop of brown hair that came down to his eyes. He was usually to be seen wearing patched blue jeans when not at school. Today was no exception.

"Joel, come and sit down and have your lunch. Where have you been? Ben has been home ages," Mr Green said, in between mouthfuls of apple crumble.

Joel put the bag on the kitchen table and sauntered into the dining room. His long fringe of hair now flopped into his eyes, looking like a waterfall coming over a cliff. He flicked his fringe out of his eyes. He was trying to look relaxed but his heart was beating fast. In his mind he was rehearsing what to say about his bike. He just wanted to blurt it out but he was sure his dad would be cross with him. Joel needed to find a way of telling him so that he didn't get into trouble.

Mrs Green slid a plate of sausage, chips and beans in front of Joel and sat down, looking at him expectantly. Joel mumbled a "thank you" and pushed his chips around with his fork.

"What's the matter? Aren't you hungry, love?" Joel's mum touched his arm as she spoke to him, but Mr Green interrupted.

"I hope you haven't been stuffing yourself with sweets again. If you have I'll..."

"Bill, please! I think there's something wrong. What is it, Joel?"

Mr Green ran his fingers through his black, bristly moustache. Joel looked down at his plate. He pushed a sausage across it with his knife. He spoke softly, not wanting to look at his mum and dad.

"I left my bike outside Baines' when I got the shopping. When I came out, someone had stolen it."

"What!" Mr Green leapt to his feet. "This is Edensbury. People don't go stealing bikes from outside shops. You did have the lock on, didn't you?"

Joel said nothing.

"You didn't? Oh no!"

"Bill. Please. Go and report it, will you?"

Mr Green went into the hall to phone the local police. Joel's mum looked at him with her warm, green eyes. She had a round face with rosy cheeks. Her shoulder-length hair was wavy and brown. Joel was nearly as tall as his mum. Mrs Green continued, "Never mind, Joel. I'm sure it will turn up. Perhaps some boys just took it for a joke."

Joel gave a weak smile and bit his bottom lip. He almost started crying again but held the tears back. "Mum, do you think you and Dad could get me a new bike? Ben's had one."

"Yes, but that was Ben's birthday present and you know he helped pay for it too. He saved for two years for that. Joel, I'm sorry. We don't have that sort of money even though we would like to give you a new bike. It's just not possible. Sorry."

Mr Green came back into the room. "They took the details. Said they'll send someone in a few days. It's obviously not a priority for them. Apparently that's the third stolen bike in a fortnight. I had no idea Edensbury had such a criminal element."

Bill Green smiled at Joel as he sat back at the table. Joel's dad was tall and thin. His hair had once been jet-black but was now mostly grey, neatly combed, with a side parting. This made him look older than he really was. "Sorry I got cross just now. It doesn't help when I lose my temper like that."

14

"That's all right, Dad. Please may I be excused? I'm not very hungry."

"Yes, OK."

Joel lay on his bed, in the room he shared with Ben. He looked at the picture of a mountain bike race on the wall. The picture was Ben's but Joel liked it too. There was so much colour in the riders' vests and helmets. The forest background was a rich green. The mixture of determination and mud on the riders' faces attracted Joel. It looked as though they were coming right out of the picture towards him as they strained towards the finish line.

He turned away from the picture towards the other wall. Tears ran down his cheek. He wished he still had his bike. He felt angry with Ben for having a new bike. He felt angry that his bike had been stolen. Now he had nothing. Joel thumped the wall with his fist. It gave out a dull thud. He quickly withdrew his hand as he felt the stab of pain.

Why shouldn't he have a bike? Did it just depend on money? His thoughts drifted to the bicycle thefts. If it was that easy for some people to get a bike, why shouldn't he have one? In his mind he pictured himself riding a new mountain bike. What did it matter how he got one?

Chapter three

Blue Monday

"Hey Joel!" a black-haired boy called as he screeched his blue and white mountain bike to a halt next to Joel. "You not cycling today?"

"What's it look like?" said Joel moodily.

Jimmy Pierce was not the most sensitive of boys. He had short, black, curly hair and wore thick black-rimmed glasses. He was very good at school-work which was surprising because he could be quite forgetful sometimes. Jimmy ignored Joel's rude remark and called to the smaller figure on a silver mountain bike who had also stopped next to him.

"Hey Andy, someone's not very happy this morning."

"Oh, Joel looks pretty normal to me," said Andy grinning. Andy was fair-haired and always had a smile for anyone. He was quite small for his age, only coming up to Joel and Jimmy's shoulder. What he lacked in height, he made up for with cheek. Andy Jones liked to tease. He did it in fun but not everybody appreciated it. Joel wasn't in the mood for it and stuck his tongue out at Andy in reply.

You might not have guessed it from their short conversation but the three were close friends. They had all grown up together, going to school in Edensbury before coming the previous September to the Middle School in Osterton. As they walked along with their bikes, Joel told them what had happened the previous Saturday.

"Hey, we could try and track down your bike for you!" Jimmy suddenly exclaimed.

"Yeah, we could look for clues and form a gang to find the criminals," joined in Andy.

Joel smiled weakly.

"You can if you like but I think I'll wait and see what the police have to say," said Joel, without any great enthusiasm.

Monday was usually a good day at school. There was Art and French which Joel liked. But today Mrs Danielle had startled Joel out of a daydream at the end of the French lesson. His picture of the French flag had barely been started. Jimmy and Andy had finished theirs. She had given him the rest to do for homework. He hoped he could do it before he went to football practice.

The day dragged. At lunchtime Joel avoided Jimmy and Andy. They played football on the playground. He stood alone at the edge of the yard. Hands in pockets, he ignored calls to join in the game.

"Come on, Joel. You can play up front." Andy shouted. The conversation was cut short as he skidded into a tackle with a boy half as big again as he was.

Joel shrugged his shoulders and shouted, "No, thanks." His words seemed to drop on the tarmac of the playground. Andy ran off after the ball. Joel moved away towards the bike sheds.

As he entered the shelter of the bike sheds, Joel noticed how quiet it was after the noise of the playground. It was good to be out of the strong wind too. Joel looked at the row of bikes of different shapes and sizes. There were some fairly old models, even older than his BMX. He half expected to see his own bike. He hadn't thought that much of it when he had it, but now it had gone... he really missed it. He felt himself getting angry with the thieves.

Joel ran his hands along the row of bikes and then stopped. His hand rested on the saddle of a purple and blue mountain bike. Joel gave a low whistle as he stepped back to admire the 18-speed indexed gears. They even had gripshift control. This was a lovely bike. Even better than Ben's. Joel would have loved a bike like this. He glanced back down the row of bikes and caught his breath as a boy entered the sheds at the bottom entrance. He ran forward with a lock in his hand.

"Hey! Green! That's my bike. Get your hands off."

"I was only looking, honest." Joel stepped back from the bike as Martin Harrison from Year 7 bent down and placed the lock around the front wheel and the steel frame of the mounting on the shed floor. There was a click as the lock snapped shut.

"Very important to lock your bike, Green. There's been too many stolen bikes lately," said Martin.

"Yes...," said Joel cautiously. "Nice bike. You had it long?"

"Christmas," replied Martin, standing up. He was a couple of inches taller than Joel and a bit heavier. Joel knew he played in the school rugby team in the forwards. Other children called him "the steamroller" or "tank man" behind his back. Although they laughed at him, most of them were afraid of Martin. Joel avoided his gaze and moved away out the top end of the bike sheds. He could hear the school bell for the end of lunch-time and jogged up to the line of chattering school children going into the Year 6 entrance. He felt relieved that Martin Harrison hadn't made more of him looking at his bike.

On his way to football practice that night, Joel walked alone down the High Street. His mum had arranged with Andy's dad for him to get a lift home. Joel felt angry that he couldn't cycle. Why couldn't he have a mountain bike? Everyone else had got one. Why was it his parents couldn't afford to buy him one? These thoughts jostled in his mind.

The prospect of the evening's football seemed

less exciting. It was now fully dark. The glare of the street lights lit up the pavement as he neared Baines' corner. Joel's heart seemed to skip a beat. Outside the supermarket he saw the same purple and blue machine he had admired in the bike sheds.

Martin Harrison must be in the shop. Joel peered into the brightly lit window, glancing down the narrow aisles as he moved towards the bike. He couldn't see Martin anywhere. Perhaps he had left his bike by accident. Maybe I could return it to him, thought Joel. He bent down by the front tyre. The gleaming aluminium wheel shone in the glare of the shop lights. No lock. Joel swallowed hard. I could ride it home, tell Mum and Dad I found it and then ride it into school for Martin tomorrow, thought Joel.

Joel Green wasn't the sort of boy to steal. He knew some older boys in Year 7 who had been caught stealing from Baines'. Shop-lifting it was called. They had been reported to the police and to the school. Joel didn't want that. But he did want a bike and some boys had stolen his. A jelly-like feeling came over his legs.

Surely that's not stealing? I would return it, thought Joel. If I could just have a little ride on it.

Joel caught his breath as he heard footsteps behind him. He froze, bent over the front tyre. Who was it?

Chapter four

Joel gets an invitation

"If I didn't know any better, I would say that was a Norman Albert special."

Joel felt himself relax a little as he heard the deep warm voice of the man behind him.

"I... I don't know," Joel cleared his throat and spoke quietly to the elderly man who stood smiling at him.

"Oh, a present, was it? Well, I don't want to spoil a secret but I'd recognise one of my bikes anywhere."

"Your bike? But I thought..."

"Well, when I said mine, I meant I had sold it. I'm Norman Albert of Albert Bikes. You know, in the High Street."

"Oh. Yes, Mr Albert. It is a lovely bike. I was just looking at it. It belongs to a friend. Well, someone from school actually and I..."

"Sorry... er,"

"Joel. Joel Green. We live on the Waverley estate."

"Sorry, Joel. I thought this was your bike."

"No. I had mine stolen last Saturday." Joel looked down at his feet.

"Stolen, you say? Oh dear, I am sorry. You know, I seem to be hearing a lot about bikes being stolen lately."

Joel felt himself relaxing. Norman Albert seemed a kind man. He wore glasses with silver rims. Joel noticed his shiny eyes and the creases in the old man's face as he smiled. Although he was very tall, he bent down towards Joel and talked with him in a way that made Joel feel comfortable.

As they stood talking by the shop doorway, an elderly lady pushed past them. "Evening Norman. Evening young Joel."

"Hello, Mrs Murdoch," said Joel. Norman Albert held the door open for the old lady. Then he picked up a Baines' basket and handed it to her.

"Thank you, Norman. Most kind."

"My pleasure, Alice." He smiled again. Then he turned again to Joel. "Now, Joel. You tell me about your bike."

He related the whole story beginning with the race in the Country Park with Ben through to how his mum and dad didn't feel able to buy him a new bike.

Norman listened attentively. At the end of Joel's story he pulled himself up to his full height and blew out his cheeks.

"Well, I don't know. You have had a rum deal.

But I'm not sure that taking the law into your own hands is the answer."

Joel gasped. How did he know? Was it that obvious? He blushed and looked up at the old man. He was surprised to see that Norman was still smiling. He wasn't cross but Joel could tell that he was serious.

"No. I guess it wasn't."

They started walking in the direction of the Falcons' football ground.

"You off to play for the Colts?" Norman asked. Joel was relieved to get off the subject of stolen bikes.

"Yes. We train every Monday. I'm not that good but I sometimes get in the team. My mate Andy, now he's good. You should see him. Hey, do you want to come and watch us, Mr Albert?"

"Norman. My friends call me Norman."

Joel laughed, "OK, Norman. Do you want to come?" They stopped by a street lamp. The old man slipped his hand inside his coat and pulled out a gold fob watch. He peered at it in the light of the street lamp.

"Thank you but no. I'm due home. I've been late at the shop. Got a special job on."

"A special job?"

"Yes. I'm building a bike for my Olympic friend. You heard of Dave Chapman?"

"You mean the mountain biker? He's the British cross country champion. He's brilliant."

Norman laughed loudly. The deep sort of laugh that makes you feel better for having done it. "That's him. Well, I'm making his bike for the British trials. He's hoping to be picked for the British team for the Olympics."

"Wow! Ben and I think he's great. Ben's my older brother. He's got a mountain bike. Not as good as the ones in your shop window, though."

"The bike I'm building for Dave couldn't be bought in a shop. There's none other like it in the whole country."

Joel stopped as they neared the football ground. He could hear the shouts of the boys as they were training.

"I've got to go now, Norman. Sorry."

"That's all right. What do you say to coming past my shop tomorrow night to see this bike? Ask your mum and dad first though."

"Oh, can I? That would be great. Yeah, I'd love to. See you." Joel scampered off towards the changing rooms.

Norman stood watching Joel run off. Suddenly he winced with pain and bent forward, folding his arms over his chest. After a moment, the old man relaxed. He stood up straight and walked off. His slow walk contrasted with Joel's excited half skip, half run. Norman wished he felt fitter. He had to finish this bike on time.

Chapter five

Custom-built

"Joel! You not feeling well? Or haven't you been to bed?" Joel looked up to see Ben's grinning face peering round the kitchen door. Ben's short blonde hair stood out from his head like bristles on a brush. He was three years older than Joel. At thirteen he behaved like he thought he was a grown up. Well, he was taller than Joel by three inches. He went to the Senior school in Osterton. He was dressed in black school trousers and a black leather jacket with the collar turned up, which covered the rest of his school uniform.

"Ha, ha. Very funny," Joel replied and continued getting his cereal. "It's you who's late for walking Digger." The boys took it in turns to walk the dog.

"Tell you what, Joel. You could do it for me and I could give you some sweets."

"No, I've got to go to school early. I want to get the first bus in."

"OK, suit yourself. Come on, Digger, let's go." Ben zipped up his jacket and put on sun-glasses, even though it was barely light outside. He slipped the lead on the little dog. Digger bounded for the door and almost got himself trapped as Ben opened it. In a moment they had both disappeared. Ben trailed after the dog shouting at him to "heel!" Joel hurried through his cereal and toast before his mum and dad appeared. Grabbing his schoolbag off the hall floor he shouted a quick "Bye!" and was out of the front door before anyone could reply.

Andy and Jimmy were waiting in the playground. The three boys liked to get to school before most people arrived. There was more room to play football in the playground for one thing. Today they didn't get as far as playing football. Andy and Jimmy were too excited.

"Joel, do you want to be part of our detective club?" asked Jimmy as they dumped their bags in the corner of the deserted playground. "We're going to investigate your bike." He pushed his glasses back up his nose with his forefinger. He wrinkled his nose as he did so, exposing his forest of freckles.

Jimmy liked clubs. He often tried to get Andy and Joel to join him in some scheme or other. Joel eyed them thoughtfully. The look on Andy's face told him that Jimmy had convinced him about the club.

"Well, you could start with Martin Harrison. He said a strange thing to me about keeping bikes locked up or they might be stolen. I felt he knew something..."

"Yeah, Martin Harrison. He could be our first suspect!" Jimmy waved his arms about as he continued, "We're going to solve the mystery of your disappearing bike. We'll get it back for you! We need to look for clues. We could start outside Baines' and..."

"I can't come," said Joel. "Sorry."

"Why not?" asked Andy. "We need you to be there."

"I've got an invitation," said Joel smugly, "to go and see an Olympic bike." He explained about the talk he had with Norman Albert. Joel hoped Andy and Jimmy might be envious.

The bell went. They hadn't noticed the school yard filling up. Joel rushed off, leaving Jimmy and Andy to arrange their first meeting of the detective club.

For the second day running, Joel didn't pay attention in class. Fortunately there was no extra work to do. Joel managed to keep on the right side of the teachers. When the school day ended, he was first in the bus queue for Edensbury. He looked forward to seeing Norman again. Although he had only just met him, he really liked the old man.

Albert's bike shop appeared different to the other shops on the High Street. The dark brown paint on the window frames and the cream paint for the sign of the shop name certainly made it seem old. The windows looked like they could do with a good clean. There was no window display to speak of. Joel noticed a pile of cycle lamps in a corner. Three bikes were pushed into the remainder of the shop window. They looked sparkling clean, almost out of place compared to the rest of the shop. Joel couldn't see anybody inside. As he pushed the door, a bell clinged somewhere towards the back. The oil-stained "Open" sign waggled as he shut the door behind him.

Inside, the smell of oil mixed with the leather smell of the bike saddles. It made Joel tingle with excitement. There was a sound of footsteps on wooden flooring from the back room. Norman appeared in the open doorway. He was wiping his hands on a rag. His dark blue overalls had an oil stain down the front. Joel noticed his silvery hair was more ruffled than when he had seen it last night. Norman peered at him over his spectacles which had slipped to the end of his nose.

"Now then, young Joel. Glad you could come." His voice was warm and welcoming. Joel relaxed. "Care for a glass of orange?"

"Oh yes, please."

"Well, come on in the back then and I'll see what I've got."

Joel followed the old man into the dimly lit room. The walls were lined with faded brown newspaper cuttings of old cycle races. The bikes in the pictures were old road racing bikes. At one end of the room was a workbench. Spanners and rags littered the bench. In the middle a space had been cleared and there was a tray looking a bit out of place. On the tray was a bottle of fizzy orange, two glasses and a plate of chocolate biscuits.

"I hoped you would come," said Norman as he offered Joel a biscuit. Joel bit into the chocolate eagerly. He was looking around expectantly, hoping to see the bike. There were one or two older bikes in the corner which were obviously being repaired but there was no sign of the Olympic bike. Norman handed him a glass of orange. Joel took a slurp and then coughed as the bubbles went up his nose. Norman laughed and patted Joel gently on the back.

"Well, I'd better let you see this bike," he said and disappeared into a side room. He reappeared a moment later, wheeling a bike, but it was covered in a brown blanket. He leaned the bike against the workbench. Then standing to one side, he pulled the corners of the blanket and whisked it off the bike like one of those magicians that you see on television.

"There! What do you think of that? 'Course it's not quite finished yet. Still got to do some work on the gears and Dave has to be measured for his saddle before it's done... Four months this has taken me so far."

Joel gasped in delight. This was better than Ben's or Martin Harrison's bikes. The racing green bike frame was covered in plastic to protect it. The transfers on the crossbar spelled out Dave

Chapman's name in silver letters. It looked a little odd without the saddle but Joel didn't mind. He was seeing a real live, hand-made, Olympic mountain bike.

"Does it take four months for you to make every bike?"

"No. This is a special one. I have to get it finished in four weeks for the trials. If I'd known it would be so hard I would have allowed six months. I don't want to let Dave down." Norman replaced the brown blanket carefully. "I've got to get on now but why don't you come again and see the bike?"

"Can I? Maybe Saturday if that's all right?"

"Well, check with your mum and dad. I'll always be glad to see you."

Joel felt that he meant it. He liked Norman.

Later that evening as he lay in bed, Joel was half asleep and half awake. Ben was in bed reading a mountain bike magazine. He was choosing a new cycle helmet from the adverts in it.

"What do you think of this one? It's really cool." Ben asked. Joel made no reply, he was nearly asleep. As he dozed he dreamed of having his own Olympic mountain bike. If only Norman Albert would build him one.

Chapter six

Lost ball

During the next two days, Jimmy and Andy spent some of their spare time on the search for Joel's bike. They were looking for clues, without success.

They waited around outside Baines' on Wednesday afternoon after school. They found there was only so long you could look at a drainpipe without getting bored. Their attempts to interview Mr Graham, the supermarket manager, were spoiled because it was his day off on Wednesday. The investigation was suspended for the day. They decided to see if Joel wanted to play football instead. Joel agreed and the three boys set off to play at their usual spot.

The old cricket ground, where they play, was the other side of Edensbury from the Waverley Estate. At one end of the ground was St Thomas' Church. When they got there, the boys ran towards the church. They used the old white cricket screen for a goal. The church clock struck four as the boys started their kick-about. Jimmy was in goal. Joel and Andy were tackling each other and trying to be the first to score three goals. Joel was "England", and Andy "Brazil". The game was going well. Jimmy had just made two good saves from Joel when Andy fired a shot high over the sight screen.

"Oh, go and get it," wailed Jimmy. "It's in the churchyard."

"No way! It came off Joel," Andy argued.

"Yeah, but it was your shot. Joel couldn't do anything about it."

Andy gave in. Jimmy and Joel watched him take a run at the stone wall surrounding the churchyard. It was about as tall as he was. Andy scrambled onto the top. There was a thud as he disappeared over the other side of the wall. Joel and Jimmy sat down on the grass and waited.

A few minutes later, Andy's muffled voice came from over the wall, "Did you see where it went? I can't find it."

Joel and Jimmy slowly got to their feet and scrambled onto the wall. From the top of the wall they could see Andy about ten metres away looking around the bottom of a beech tree. The yard was full of gravestones. Some were in orderly rows, like soldiers at attention. Some were almost falling over. There were grey headstones covered in dark green moss. Some headstones were of new white marble.

Jimmy gave a shudder. "I think we should leave the ball if we can't see it."

"It's all right for you to say that. It's *my* ball,"

grumbled Andy, still looking round the tree.

Joel slipped off the top of the wall into the graveyard. He moved quietly and cautiously among the graves. Over to their right, Joel noticed a mound of freshly dug earth. He and Andy went over to it. "Found it!" shouted Joel as he disappeared behind the mound. Jimmy jumped down from the wall and ran to join the others. Next to the mound was a gleaming white headstone. Joel bent down to look at it. "Hey! This is brand new." said Joel. He read from the gravestone, "*Lord, we commit your servant Edith to your loving care...*" Joel frowned. "Wonder what that means?"

"Come on, let's go! I've got the ball now," said Andy.

"Yeah," said Jimmy quickly. "We don't want to get caught in here."

The boys walked out across the cricket field. It was nearly their tea-time so the game was abandoned. They said little to each other on the way home. Jimmy felt he didn't want to see another grave for a long time. Andy was dreaming of Edensbury Colt's next game away to Makerley Town.

Joel couldn't stop thinking about the grave in the church yard. He wondered about the old lady. Where was she? Was she in the ground? Did she stay there for ever?

After tea when Ben had left the table, Joel asked

his mum and dad, "What happens when you die?"

Joel's dad stroked his moustache thoughtfully for a minute after Joel had asked his question.

"I think that everybody who dies goes to a place called paradise."

"Well, what's paradise like?" Joel asked.

"Well, I don't think anybody really knows, Joel. What do you think, Jen?"

"I believe in heaven, the place your dad called paradise, but I'm not sure that everybody goes there. I think we have to have lived a good life first. I remember your grandmother was very sure that she would go to heaven. She said that because she loved Jesus, when she died she would be with him for ever in heaven. The older she got, the more certain she became, even when she was very sick at the end of her life. I wish I had her faith."

As he lay in bed that night, Joel hoped the lady who had died had believed in Jesus like his grandma. He didn't like the thought of her lying dead in the ground. He thought about what his mum had said about his grandma. If she had been alive he felt sure he could have asked her about Jesus and heaven. He pushed the thought out of his mind for the moment. Now there was Saturday to look forward to. The events of the afternoon were fading. In his mind he pictured Dave Chapman's bike. Would Norman get it finished in time?

Chapter seven

Joel gets a better invitation

Joel lay sleepily in the warmth of his bed. He became aware of a scratching noise. His heart gave a jump. He sat up in bed. The scratching continued. It was coming from the door. Joel went to open it.

"Oh Digger! What are you doing?" The little spaniel bounded into the room. Joel noticed Ben's empty bed and then remembered that Ben was doing something with the Scouts that Saturday morning. At last it was Saturday, the day he was going back to Albert's bike shop.

"Have to be a quick walk after breakfast today, old boy. Sorry." Digger shuffled round Joel's feet, getting in the way as Joel tried to get dressed. He loved being with Joel. Ben didn't seem to have as much time for Digger these days but Joel always made a fuss of him.

Joel gave Digger his walk after breakfast. They went only as far as the football ground and back, a twenty minute walk. Joel's mum gave him a list of groceries to get from Baines' after he had been to

Albert's. She told him to be home by twelve as lunch was going to be early. They were all due to go over to Makerley to see Uncle Jeff and Aunt Linda. Joel groaned quietly to himself. His mum knew this would not be one of his favourite afternoons. Still, he had the visit to the bike shop to look forward to.

Joel felt the wind on his face as he left his house. The alley-way leading to the High Street gave some much needed shelter. It wasn't raining but the dark clouds moving quickly in the sky made Joel think rain was likely. He was glad to be going indoors.

As he reached Albert's, he noticed Norman was serving a customer. He looked up from the counter as the bell tinged. Joel quietly closed the door and stood just inside the shop.

"Won't be a minute, Joel. Do you want to go through?"

"OK. Hi, Paul." Joel smiled at the customer who turned and recognised him. It was Paul Davis from Year 9 at school.

Joel went into the back room. He stared a bit closer at the faded cuttings on the wall. One headline read: "Albert triumphs in Milk Race". There was a picture of a much younger looking Norman Albert in vest and shorts with a sash round him and a big silver cup in his hand.

Joel turned as Norman entered the room. "What's the Milk Race?"

Norman smiled. "Do you really want to know?" Seeing Joel's eager expression, he continued, "Well, it was the biggest road race held in Britain. Used to be known throughout the world as a tough competition. It was the British Championship of road racing. I won it once. Had my picture in the paper as you can see." Joel could tell the old man was pleased at his interest. "The race took place over a few weeks. A bit like the Tour de France that you see now on television, but in those days we didn't have all the back-up crew the riders have today. When you come another time I'll show you the cup I won, if you like. It's locked away so I can't get it for you now but next time maybe."

Norman moved over to the bench. Today there was a flask on the little tray with two mugs and a plate of bourbon biscuits. Norman poured two cups of steaming milky cocoa from the flask. He gave one to Joel and offered him the plate of biscuits. The two of them sat on some high backed stools that Norman kept by his workbench. As he eased himself on to the stool, Joel saw Norman wince with pain.

"You all right, Norman?" Joel asked.

"Oh yes. Just a bit of chest pain. Heartburn or something. My wife says it's because I eat my food too fast." He laughed as he said this. His kindly face relaxed into a smile. Joel felt happier.

"How's Dave's bike coming along?"

"Not as fast as I'd hoped, Joel. To be honest, I wish I had a bit more time. It's the gears you see. Got to get them just right. Dave needs the best on the bike. I've ordered the gears specially from Italy. They haven't come yet and time is running out." Joel noticed that Norman's face had gone rather pale at this last comment. He ran his fingers through his silvery hair and sucked in his cheeks. "If they don't come soon, I'm going to let Dave down. I couldn't bear to think of it..."

Norman disappeared into the little side room where he kept Dave's bike. When he reappeared, pushing the bike, Joel noticed the new saddle wrapped in polythene. There was a space on the handlebars where the gripshift gears were to go. Joel hoped they would come soon.

Joel ran his hands over the special blackwall tyres on the bike. The ridges seemed firm and strong. He thought again how he would like a bike of his own. He had planned to ask Norman to make him one and pay for it week by week. He couldn't ask him, not now, it would be too selfish. He saw how tense Norman was at getting this bike finished. Norman seemed such a kind man.

"Do you like the saddle?" Norman patted it in the same way Joel sometimes patted Digger. Joel could see Norman was pleased with his work. "Dave is coming in on Wednesday to have a fitting. Do you want to come along? He's not expected until four o'clock so you'll have finished school by then. I'm sure he won't mind. And you can see him on TV before then."

"TV?" Joel's eyes lit up.

"Yes, on the Monday evening local news programme. He's had a camera crew following him for the last day or so. They are filming him at an event today down south. Just a shame that my bike won't be featured, but come the Olympic Trial hopefully it will..."

"Can I talk to him? On Wednesday – when he comes?"

"Course you can. You're always welcome, Joel. I'll look forward to introducing you to Dave."

"Thanks. See you Wednesday then." Joel beamed at Norman, then turned and left the shop. He sped along the High Street to Baines' corner. Such a difference from the previous Saturday. Now he had a meeting with Dave Chapman to look forward to. Perhaps Dave would give him some tips on trials riding? Joel was looking forward to Wednesday so much that even the thought of visiting Uncle Jeff and Aunt Linda didn't seem so bad.

Aunt Linda had made a fuss. She always did when the Greens came. Joel and Ben were dressed in their best clothes – not something they were used to on a Saturday afternoon.

Tea was good. Joel loved Aunt Linda's salmon sandwiches. They never had salmon sandwiches at home. Joel thought it made up for getting dressed up.

The car journey home began uneventfully. Joel leaned forward and pressed his nose against the cold window and watched the street lights going by. His mop-like fringe made a mark on the steamed up car window.

As they left Makerley it began to rain. After a few minutes, Joel could hear the swishing of the wheels going through the puddles. The rain got heavier as they neared home. Joel listened to his parents' conversation in the front seat. They were obviously worried about the weather getting worse. The wiper blades on the front window were going at double speed. Mr Green was leaning forward, screwing up his eyes to try to see through the windscreen.

"Don't you think we should stop, Bill, until this storm goes off?" Mrs Green asked anxiously.

"No need to worry, Jen. It will be all right. We are nearly at Edensbury."

Joel thought he knew where they were. They had just passed the entrance to the Country Park at Osterton on the back road to Edensbury. They would soon be home.

Suddenly Mr Green was braking. There was a squeal from the tyres. Mr Green was fighting with the steering wheel. The car was skidding sideways across the road onto the grass verge. The tyres squealed. Mrs Green shouted, "Bill! Watch out!"

Chapter eight

Football in heaven

Silence followed. Joel noticed the engine had stopped. His heart was thumping. He swallowed hard. Mr Green was sitting stiffly in his seat, staring through the windscreen. He suddenly relaxed.

"Is everyone all right? I'm sorry. Something ran across the road and I swerved to miss it. A fox or a dog – don't know which. Didn't mean to scare you."

"Bill! You could have killed us! Please take it easy." Mrs Green's voice was trembling. Joel had never heard her sound so scared. Did she really mean that we might have been killed? thought Joel. Would I be going to heaven? He didn't speak his thoughts out loud.

He didn't say anything more that evening. When they got home, Mr Green said sorry to everyone again for the near accident. Mrs Green was able to laugh about it. Ben was looking forward to telling his school mates on Monday about the "smash" his dad nearly had.

Next day, Joel decided he would call for Andy and Jimmy. He felt sure they would want to inspect the skid site with him. He was right. Joel plucked up the courage to ask Ben if he could borrow his new bike. Ben very kindly said "Yes" on condition that Joel would ask if he could meet Dave on Wednesday as well. Joel was warned several times by his mum not to damage Ben's bike. At last he was on his way to Osterton with his two friends.

Jimmy and Andy had some news on the BMX investigation. They had kept watch outside Martin Harrison's house the previous afternoon.

"You'll never guess what we saw," said Jimmy. Martin Harrison was wheeling a bike out of his house. A man took it from him and put it into a van. We got the registration number..."

"Was it my bike?" Joel interrupted.

"No. Sorry, Joel," Jimmy continued, "but it wasn't his new mountain bike either."

"The man gave him some money! We think he could be part of a bike smuggling gang!" joined in Andy.

Jimmy and Andy told Joel their plans for the investigation. They would widen the search to include Martin's school friends. Joel was still not keen to be involved. He was more interested in Dave Chapman's bike.

The boys arrived at the entrance to the country park. A few cars were turning in at the park gates — families out for a Sunday morning walk. After a few minutes of looking, they settled on what Joel thought was the skid site. There were tyre tracks on the grass verge where the car had skidded to a halt. The boys spent a few more minutes looking around. There wasn't really much to see but they enjoyed being at the scene of a real "near accident".

Eventually they set off, cycling back to Edensbury on the cycle path that ran alongside the main road. They liked to race on the fast stretch near the outskirts of Edensbury. As usual, Joel won.

The boys cycled in single file past the cricket ground and then stopped by the church. Joel planned that they would cut back through the woods from there so they could do some 'off road' riding. He was about to lead them round to the track that went through the woods, when he noticed a familiar figure, dressed in a grey overcoat and flat cap, standing on the church path. It was Norman. He was talking quietly with a couple of ladies that Joel didn't know. A few other people filed past the boys on their way out of church. Joel shouted to Jimmy and Andy, "Hey! Wait! There's someone I want to speak to. It's Norman Albert."

"Who's he?" asked Jimmy as he pulled up alongside Joel.

"He's the man who owns the bike shop."

"Can we say hello to him too?" asked Andy.

"Yeah. Sure."

Eventually the conversation on the church path ended and Norman waved goodbye to the ladies.

He caught sight of the boys outside the gate and came over to speak to them. Joel noticed he was walking slowly and that he was bent over a little. Joel thought Norman looked tired and pale but he still smiled warmly at them.

"You three out to capture Dave Chapman's title then?" Norman laughed as he spoke. Jimmy and Andy looked puzzled. Joel hadn't talked much about Dave Chapman to them, so he briefly reminded them about Norman building Dave a bike for the Olympic trial. He also told them that Dave was going to come to the shop on Wednesday for a fitting.

When they heard this, Jimmy and Andy both wanted to come to the shop on Wednesday. Norman agreed, provided it was all right with their parents. He also said that Ben could come too. The two boys quickly said goodbye and rushed off in the direction of their homes. Norman smiled. "Good to see they are so keen. Perhaps we'll get a few more Olympic hopefuls around here."

From where they stood talking, Joel could see into the churchyard. He looked over to the gleaming white headstone with writing on it. Several bunches of flowers were laid by the headstone. Some of the petals were dropping off and lay on top of the newly laid turf that covered the grave. Norman noticed Joel staring past him. "What's the matter?" he asked.

Joel explained about the football going into the

churchyard by the grave. Norman laughed. "I wonder if we'll be able to play football in heaven?"

Joel asked him, "What happens when you die?"

Norman looked at him, "That's a good question but it's a hard one!" he said. "I don't think anyone really knows until they die, but I believe God has given us some help in the Bible so that we can understand part of it." Joel waited while Norman stopped to think. He was pleased that his friend thought it was a good question.

The old man spoke softly and quietly but firmly. He continued, "Our bodies are getting older and more worn out all the time. Especially mine! There will come a time when our bodies will give out and we die. But there is a part of us that God has made that will not wear out and die. That part, some people call it our spirit, will live for ever."

Norman could see that Joel found this hard to understand. He smiled and went on, "Think of it like this. What makes a good mountain bike? It's not the frame or the wheels. It's the design. The design is the essential part of the bike. That's what makes the bike special. You can't touch the design or ride on it but it is there. The bike can be destroyed but because the design remains it can be rebuilt with new materials. You will then have the same bike. Now, what if the bike were rebuilt with everlasting parts? Then you'd have the same bike but one that lasts for ever. And that is what I believe God does with us when we die. We get a new body that can last for ever."

Joel still looked thoughtful.

Norman pointed to the graveyard. "So when we die, the worn out body gets buried in the ground and stays there. Our spirit gets a new body and lives for ever. We will either be with God or not, depending on whether we have followed God's way."

"What does 'following God's way' mean?" interrupted Joel.

"Well, I always think of our lives as being like a bike race. There are many routes to take to the finish but only one, which is God's way, guarantees a win. The other routes belong to God's enemy. Christians are those who follow God's route. They trust God and ask him to show them how to live. They go to heaven when life's journey ends. Some people follow God's enemy. They are not with God when they die. Sadly, they are apart from God for ever in a place some people call hell. Everyone has to choose which route to take."

Joel listened carefully. The answer Norman gave was much clearer than his mum and dad had managed. He wondered how Norman could know all that.

"Does that answer your question, Joel?"

Joel nodded. "I think so."

"Well, I've got to get home for lunch. My wife will wonder where I've got to. See you Wednesday." Norman turned to go.

"Do you think there will be...?" Joel shouted after his friend.

"What?"

"Football. You know, in heaven?"

Norman turned back and smiled at Joel. "Heaven is a happy place. If football makes you happy then I'm sure it will be there. I'm looking forward to a bit of cycling myself."

Chapter nine

The TV show

In the playground on Monday morning, Jimmy and Andy and a few other friends were huddled in the corner by the bike sheds.

"We're going to meet him," Jimmy was saying, as Joel wandered up to the group.

"Meet who?" Joel asked.

"Dave Chapman. We're allowed to." Andy joined in. The other boys looked enviously at Jimmy and Andy who were being given the chance to meet a local hero.

"Do you think he'll win a medal?" asked one boy, also called Dave.

"Bound to," said Jimmy, "but he's got to get through the trial first."

"My dad doesn't think he's got a chance." The group turned round to see the bulky figure of Martin Harrison standing with his hands in his pockets, chewing gum and looking at them. They all went quiet. They didn't want to argue with Martin. "Me and my dad know loads about bikes," he boasted. "Dad says I could beat Dave Chapman even if I was riding an old BMX!"

The sound of the school bell stopped Martin's boasting. Morning break was over. As they moved away from Martin, Jimmy pulled on Andy's arm.

"See! I told you Harrison is in on this!" Jimmy said in a loud whisper. Andy nodded.

"You two any nearer to finding my BMX?" asked Joel. "I hope you are because I'd love to get my bike back."

As they neared the entrance, Joel stopped Andy and Jimmy. "Hey! Don't forget to watch Dave on TV tonight."

'Oh, we can't," said Andy. "It's training tonight. The Makerley game is less than two weeks away and we want to be in the team."

"My mum's going to video it," added Jimmy.

Joel couldn't imagine why they didn't want to see the programme live. What if the video didn't record properly? They might miss it.

Joel's dad was home from work early on that Monday evening. He surprised the family by coming through the door just in time for the local news on TV. He wouldn't admit that he had come home especially to watch the programme but Joel had noticed him taking an interest in reports about Dave Chapman ever since Joel had first gone to Albert's to see the bike.

Mr Green sank into the chair by the fire with a loud sigh. He didn't even bother to take off the grey jacket of his business suit. The opening credits for the news programme were just coming onto the screen. Mrs Green put a tray with a plate of steak and kidney pie, mashed potatoes and peas in front of him. He muttered a "thank you" and began eating whilst keeping his eyes fixed firmly on the screen.

The whole family was sitting in the lounge watching. Mr Green had been the only person interested in the news item which dealt with a new treatment for greenfly developed by a local garden centre. A loud chorus of "Shhhhh!" stopped him mid-sentence as he was telling Joel's mum all about how it would help his roses.

The story about Dave was introduced over a picture of him winning the Northern championships last year. The picture showed him leaning forward over the handlebars, gritting his teeth in a sort of half grin. You could just make out his ginger hair under his purple helmet. The rest of his face and most of his black and green outfit were covered in spots of mud.

"Hey! That looks like the poster on my wall!" shouted Ben, pointing at the screen.

There followed some action footage of Dave competing in Middle Marsh at the weekend. Joel remembered that Norman had mentioned that there would be a crew filming Dave at a race down south. The series of shots on the screen had been taken beside a hummock in the forest track. Joel and Ben gasped as the bikes appeared to fly high into the air. They were going past so fast that Joel couldn't tell which one was Dave. The commentator was saying that Dave had finished second. This was after he had come off his bike at a tight bend on the course. So in fact second was a good result for him.

The final part of the report was an interview with Dave. Joel liked Dave instantly. He looked like a runner, dressed in his British team tracksuit top. He laughed and joked with the interviewer. The interviewer asked,

"The Olympics are only a few months away, Dave. How important is it to you to win a medal?"

Dave smiled, "Well, I'll have to make the team first. The trials are coming up soon. Obviously I want to do well: to get in the team, to compete for my country, to win a medal. These are all important things. As a Christian, I pray to be successful in the races, but being successful isn't everything. An Olympic medal isn't the most important thing for me. I want to live my life God's way. That may include winning a medal. It may not."

The report on Dave finished as suddenly as it had begun. Mr Green turned the TV set off. There was silence for a moment. Ben was the first to speak. "There weren't many pictures of the bikes. I wanted to see more."

"What did you think of it, Jen?" Mr Green asked Joel's mum.

"I enjoyed it. He looked younger than I thought he would be. He spoke really well, though. It must be lovely to have a faith like that, Bill. He was very brave to say that Christianity was more important to him than winning an Olympic medal."

"Yes... " replied Mr Green thoughtfully.

Mrs Green collected up the dinner things. Joel wasn't noticed as he slipped out of the room to go upstairs.

Later he lay on his bed, looking up at the ceiling. How can anything be more important than an Olympic medal? Joel thought about the TV report. He had enjoyed seeing Dave in the race at Middle Marsh. He looked forward to Wednesday. He still had no bike of his own but that did not seem so important now. He had his friend Norman and he and Ben were going to meet Dave Chapman.

Maybe Dave would take me to one of his races, thought Joel. He didn't know if this would happen. If he had known what other events were to take place before he saw Dave race, he might not have looked forward to it so keenly.

Chapter ten

The boys meet Dave

The familiar "ting" of the shop bell sounded as Joel barged into the shop.

"That you, Joel?" Norman's voice appeared to come from the back room. "Come through, son."

Joel rushed through the doorway. He stopped as he saw Norman. He still looked very tired and pale. He was leaning against the bench, not in his usual overalls. He was wearing a red and yellow checked waistcoat over a dark green shirt. Joel hadn't seen him looking so brightly dressed before. The bright colours only seemed to emphasise the paleness of his face, though. Norman pulled his gold watch from his pocket. It was attached to the waistcoat by a long gold chain.

"Dave's not due for a quarter of an hour yet. Are Ben and your friends coming?"

"Yes. They'll be along on the next bus. I was fastest out of school today. I caught the first bus."

Joel noticed Dave's bike leaning against one wall, covered by the same blanket he had seen before. Joel didn't dare ask if it was finished.

"Did you see the programme on Dave?" asked Joel.

"Yes. He spoke very well. Shame he didn't win at Middle Marsh."

Joel's attention was taken from the bike by a suitcase that Norman had on the bench beside him.

"Here. I've got something to show you," Norman said, as he began to open the dark brown case. The gold-coloured clasp was rusty. The case clicked open and Norman lifted the lid. Inside was a large object wrapped in a yellow duster. He pulled back the cloth to reveal a silver cup. It was the same one Joel had seen in the photograph on the wall.

"There. What do you think about that?" Norman was smiling as he pulled the cup from the case. He held it up above his left shoulder, just like he was doing in the photograph. Joel thought he still looked like a champion.

"Is winning that race the best thing you've ever done?" Joel asked.

"In racing? Yes." He paused. "But there are more important things than winning trophies and races."

"Dave said the same thing on TV," said Joel. "What did he mean?"

"Well, to a Christian, being a friend of God is the most important thing in our lives. A trophy is not for ever. Even the memory of a victory can fade. But knowing God is something that can always be fresh and exciting."

Joel was puzzled. He'd always thought there could be nothing better than winning a gold medal or a silver cup and beating everyone else.

His thoughts were stopped by the sound of the shop bell. Ben, Jimmy and Andy had arrived. Norman shuffled through to the front of the shop to greet them. Joel heard him explain that Dave was not yet here but he was expected any minute. Soon they were shown into the back room. The boys had the same bright-eyed look as Joel had when he first came to visit Norman.

"Wow! Jimmy, have you seen these pictures?" said Andy.

"Yeah. They're all of you, Mr Albert, aren't they?"

"You should get Norman to show you his trophy for winning the milk race." said Joel.

"Oh, can we?" asked Jimmy.

Norman smiled and opened the case again. "This is a real treat, you know. There aren't many people who get to see this trophy. Only my special friends." The boys beamed with pride at being counted as friends of the old man. They edged forward round the case and looked at their reflections in the large bowl of the cup. They were each allowed to hold it, and they passed it around like footballers at the cup final.

The celebration was cut short by the sound of the shop door being opened. Norman hurriedly put the cup back in its case and shut the lid. He disappeared into the shop. The boys could hear another man's voice. It must be Dave. They held their breath and listened. The men were coming through to the back. Joel's mouth felt dry.

Norman came through first. "Now I've got some special friends for you to meet. They've been very interested in you and this bike." Norman stepped aside and there was Dave. Joel thought he looked taller than he had imagined he would be. The smile was the same, though. Dave's ginger hair was closely cropped, which emphasised his rugged face. He was wearing a green and black track suit top.

"Norman tells me you guys might want a race?"

"Yeah. Can we?" the boys chorused. Joel forgot for a moment that he wouldn't have anything to race on. Ben wanted to tell Dave about his own bike, but seeing Joel's expression, decided to say nothing.

"Well, we'll have to see." Dave was laughing. "But once I get this bike that Mr Albert has built, you'll have a job to catch me!" He turned to Norman. "How is it coming along?"

Joel held his breath but Norman was smiling.

"All finished as promised," he said. "I had to wait for the gears to come through but they arrived by special delivery yesterday. I had to work a little late to get it finished but it's done now."

"How late?" Joel noticed the concern in Dave's

voice.

"Late enough. But it's done now." Norman moved over to the bike. He removed the blanket, more slowly than he had done last time. Dave moved forward and touched the saddle lovingly. He then crouched down to check the gears and the chain.

"Norman, this looks good. You couldn't have had much time to get these gears right but they look great." He stood up again and turned to Norman and the boys. "If this doesn't help me in the trial, I don't know what will."

Joel and the boys crowded round for a closer look. Dave and Norman stood slightly away from the chattering group. Dave was asking Norman if he could take the bike today because he wanted to start testing right away. Norman agreed, provided the saddle fitting was all right.

Norman went off to a side room and came out with a tray of fizzy drinks and a large chocolate cake.

"Celebration!" he said, passing round the tray to Dave and the boys. When each had got a glass in his hand, Norman raised his and said, "A toast. To the next Olympic champion. To Dave."

Dave laughed. The boys all copied Norman and then tucked into the drinks and cake. There was a lot of excitement in the room. Norman was quiet, relieved that his job was nearly finished.

"You know, you should get some rest, Norman.

You've earned it." Dave put his arm on Norman's shoulder. Joel noticed again how tired Norman looked. Working late and the pressure of finishing the bike in time had made him quite run down.

"Yes. You're right, Dave. Perhaps I'll take tomorrow off but I can't rest too long. I've got other customers besides you. Just as well they are not all as demanding as you are, though." He smiled.

Dave made as if to punch him in the ribs but then grabbed the man and gave him a big hug instead. "Thank you, Norman. I really appreciate what you have done. You will come and see me try it out, won't you? In Osterton on Saturday morning. You boys can come too if you like. Only don't tell the press because this bike needs to be kept secret until the Olympic trials. I don't want anybody copying it."

Joel and his friends jumped up and down in excitement. They would love to be there on Saturday. Norman smiled. He had got this far with the bike, he didn't want to miss the trials either. He hoped the bike would perform well. On Saturday they would all find out.

Chapter eleven

Where is Norman?

On Saturday Joel was grateful that Digger hadn't made a fuss as he ate his early breakfast. Ben plodded into the kitchen looking like he was still asleep. He shook his head when Joel offered him a piece of bread. "You know I'm not coming back with you?" yawned Ben as he put his jacket on. "I'm going into Osterton to see a film. Mum knows about it."

"OK," replied Joel, "but hurry up now or we'll miss the bus."

They hurried from the house and met Jimmy and Andy at the bus stop in the High Street. On the way to the Country Park, Jimmy told Joel more about their investigation. "We followed Martin Harrison and his friend, George Holland home from school yesterday. We waited outside George's house for ages. After about an hour, Martin went home. No sign of your bike Joel. Sorry."

Joel gave a half smile. He was glad the boys wanted to help find his BMX but he remembered that there had been no word from the police about it. They said that because the bike wasn't security coded it was unlikely to be found. PC Dimbleby had thought it might have been resprayed and sold, perhaps in another town.

The four boys were the only people to get off at the Country Park. It was a quarter to eight. Dave had said he would meet them at eight fifteen. He wanted to test the bike early in the morning before the park got too busy. As the boys walked down the forest road past the park ranger's cabin they could see a white transit van parked at the side of the road a little further on. The sides of the van had Dave Chapman's name printed in red and black letters. Apart from a little mud which had sprayed up behind the front wheels, the rest of the van was gleaming white. It shone out against the grey-green forest behind.

Dave greeted the boys warmly. He was dressed in a bright yellow and black singlet with black cycle shorts which almost came down to his knees. He had black cycling shoes on and was carrying his purple helmet. Another man, about Dave's age, was lifting the bike from the van. Dave introduced the man as "Pete the Mechanic". The boys crowded around Dave as he took control of the bike. He wheeled it to a nearby oak tree and leaned it against the thick gnarled trunk. Ben walked over to it for a closer look.

"Have you had a go yet, Dave?" Joel asked.

"Not yet, but we'll soon see what she can do. I'll wait until Norman gets here. I wouldn't want him to miss it."

The boys looked back up the forest road. No sign of Norman. Instead they saw a group of about twelve children entering the park gates. Behind them, the Edensbury bus was just pulling away.

"Who are this lot, then?" Dave asked with a broad grin. "It had better not be the press."

Jimmy and Andy blushed and looked uneasy. Jimmy spoke first.

"We hope you don't mind. We told a few of our school friends. We didn't mean to. It just came out. It doesn't matter, does it?"

Joel scowled at Jimmy. How could he let the secret out? Would Dave be angry?

Dave was still smiling. "No harm done, I suppose. If this bike is as good as Norman led me to believe, the opposition won't be able to do anything, even if they do hear about it before the trials. So don't worry, Jimmy."

Jimmy smiled gratefully and ran off in the direction of the approaching group. He wanted to let them know that he had managed to fix it with Dave so that they could watch the secret bike test. Dave looked at his watch. Nearly twenty to nine. It was not like Norman to be late.

At a quarter to nine, Dave mounted the saddle. "I can't wait for Norman any longer. You boys will have to tell him the details of the test when he comes." After clipping his shoes into the fittings on the pedals, Dave stood up in the saddle as he moved off onto the track.

"Right Pete, you time me. I'll do three laps of the forest. Give me the split times for each lap after I finish. Ready. Go!"

Dave sped off. The tyres crackled on the forest track. The bike weaved from side to side as he gathered speed. Dave soon disappeared from view.

"How long will he take?" Joel asked Pete.

"Not long, knowing Dave. About four minutes twenty seconds for each lap on his old bike but we're hoping he can improve on that with the new one."

The boys chattered excitedly amongst themselves for a few minutes. After what seemed like half an hour they let out a big cheer as Dave swept into view by the ranger's cabin. He sped past the group in a blur and disappeared out of sight down the track.

"How long?" Joel asked Pete.

Pete looked thoughtful. "Four minutes thirty-five seconds. I wonder if something is wrong."

Joel kept glancing back towards the entrance of the Park hoping to see Norman. There was no sign. Soon Dave reappeared. "Four fifteen," shouted Pete, "that's better."

There were more cheers and then he vanished again.

Silence fell on the group of children. Pete

looked down at the watch. Another good time would mean the bike really was a winner. Everyone realised the importance of this last lap for Dave's hopes of doing well in the trials. Joel hoped Norman would come soon.

"Come on, Dave! Come on!" Jimmy and Andy were jumping up and down as Dave appeared for the final time. Dave shot past the group. Pete clicked the watch. He punched the air.

"Yes! Four minutes five seconds!" The children all ran to Dave as he pushed the bike back to the group. They were all talking at once. Dave was nodding and smiling as he removed his helmet. He looked anxiously at Pete.

"Good," said Pete. "Very good. Bit of a blip on the first lap but the other two were smashing. I think old Norman has got you a very special machine."

Dave was panting hard. "Great. I just wish he could have been here to see it. Where is he?"

Joel stood a little back from the group. He felt sad and cross with Norman. Didn't he care about Dave and the bike? Perhaps he had been delayed at the shop instead of coming here. Joel decided he would go to see Norman on the way home and tell him all about the successful test.

Joel looked across at Dave. He was surrounded by Ben, Jimmy, Andy and the other children. They had him signing autographs and posing for photographs. Pete was bent over the bike, cleaning mud off the alloy rims with a rag. Joel called to Jimmy and Andy that he was going but they didn't seem to hear him. Dave half smiled and waved at him, but then he was distracted by another question from one of the group. Joel walked slowly away.

Joel went through what he would say to Norman when he saw him. He was not going to be rude but he felt Norman had let Dave down. He liked Norman too much to hurt him. All the same, he hoped he had a good reason for not coming this morning.

The first few shoppers were out in Edensbury High Street as Joel got off the bus. He felt his stomach tighten as he approached Albert's shop. He leant against the old shop door, grabbed the handle and pushed. It didn't move. Joel rubbed his shoulder as he stepped back from the door. The shop was all in darkness. The oily sign in the shop door window said, "Closed". There was no familiar ting of the bell. No smell of oil. No welcoming smile. Strange.

Where had Norman gone?

Chapter twelve

The notice on the door

"He must have had a good reason," Dad said to Joel at breakfast next morning. "Don't worry about it, son. You know how Norman felt about Dave. He had spent months on that bike, getting it just right. Maybe he couldn't face the chance of the bike not doing as well as he hoped."

"But why wasn't he at the shop? I went by there three times yesterday and it was all shut up. Why would he just go away like that?"

"I don't know, Joel."

Mum began to clear the breakfast things. Joel pushed his half-eaten bowl of cereal towards her.

"Not hungry. Sorry."

He went back to his room. He picked up the scrapbook he had been keeping on Dave Chapman. He had glued in several cuttings from the local papers on Dave. There were even a couple from the national papers. As Joel gazed at the pages his thoughts went back to yesterday. The new bike was fast. He thought about Dave. How good he was not to make a fuss when the gang from school turned up. How kind he was with them all. Joel hoped that Dave had at least spoken to Norman by now so he would know the bike was a success.

"Maybe Norman will be at church again. If I could get out I could go and meet him." Joel didn't feel he could go into the church because he and his family hardly ever went. He would never go in on his own. Norman had told him how he often went to church. He said he liked to feel close to God.

Later that morning, Joel was downstairs, looking through his scrapbook on Dave Chapman. Ben was upstairs doing his homework. Dad was pacing up and down in the kitchen. Joel could hear him talking to Mum.

"It's usually here by now, Jen. Where can the girl have got to?"

"Don't worry, Bill. It's only a newspaper. You can do without for one day, can't you?"

"It's Sunday, though. You know I like the papers on Sunday."

"Well, ring the shop and ask them to send one round. She has obviously missed us out."

Joel overheard the conversation and, seizing his chance, bounded into the kitchen.

"Hasn't the paper come? I'll go and get you one if you like, Dad."

"Thank you, Joel. That's very kind but it's raining. It's easier for me to phone and get them to bring one round."

"No! No, I'll go. I won't get too wet. I'll take Digger. You won't mind an extra walk, will you boy?"

Digger flicked his tail hopefully. He wouldn't get out of the basket until the lead came out but this was at least promising.

"OK. Take Digger, but don't be too long or the paper won't be worth reading."

Joel got ready quickly. Digger was bounding around by now. His enthusiasm was squashed a little by the rain outside but he was soon trotting along by Joel's side as they headed for the High Street.

Albert's shop was still shut up. Joel sped past with Digger. He quickly got the newspaper from the newsagent's. He stuffed the paper up his coat front to stop it getting wet. Digger was looking a little bedraggled when Joel untied him from the drainpipe outside the shop. Digger turned hopefully in the direction of home, but instead Joel set off to the other end of town – towards the church.

The rain was still falling. The church clock showed five to twelve. Joel and Digger sheltered under the covered gateway at the end of the path to the church door. They could hear the organ playing. There was the muffled sound of people singing. The rain spattered noisily off nearby trees onto the roof of the gateway. Joel felt wet and cold. He hoped the service would soon end.

As the clock struck twelve the big church door

opened. The vicar stood by the door, his white and black robes flapping round his legs in the wind. He held a black umbrella in his left hand and shook hands with people coming out of church with his right. He kept having to break off from the handshakes to control the umbrella which was turning inside out in the wind.

Joel tried to see if Norman was coming out. There were three or four families and several older people. Joel recognised the two ladies Norman had been talking to last week. No one spoke to him as they came past. There was no sign of Norman. After a few minutes, the vicar took down his umbrella and disappeared inside the church. The door closed with a thud.

Joel and Digger trooped home. The rain began to soak through Joel's coat. There was a big patch of wet on his chest and shoulders. Joel could feel the wet edges of the newspaper under his jacket. Dad was not going to be pleased.

It turned out Dad was so relieved at getting his paper that he didn't ask why Joel had been so long. Neither did he ask why his paper was so wet.

At school next day there was even more talk of Dave Chapman than there had been before the TV show. Some of the children already had their photos of him from Saturday's test. Dave was smiling broadly with his thumbs up in one of them. The new bike could just be seen in the background.

Several of the children were showing off Dave's autograph. Joel pretended to take an interest but really he was still thinking of Norman.

After tea, Joel got ready for football practice. As he had missed last week he had little hope of getting into the team for the Makerley game on Saturday. He still liked to go training as it was such good fun. Joel decided to go past Albert's shop again, just in case he was working late. Nothing could have prepared Joel for what he found when he got to the shop.

The High Street was deserted. Piles of rubbish from the shops lined the road ready for collection. Joel stood alone outside Albert's bike shop door. The oily "Closed" sign had been removed. In its place was a handwritten notice. Joel's heart was thumping in his chest as he read :

ALBERT'S BIKES

It is with regret that I have to announce
the death of Norman Albert.
The shop will be closed until further notice.
Sorry for any inconvenience caused.

Mrs Jean Albert

Joel must have stood silently looking at the notice for several minutes. He then became aware of someone at his shoulder.

"Oh no. Poor thing." Mrs Murdoch's voice trembled as she read the notice out loud. "Oh. What a thing to happen. I hope Jean is all right." She shuffled away down the High Street towards Baines', towing her shopping trolley.

Joel ran home. There didn't seem any point in going to football now.

Chapter thirteen

A sad day

Mum had given him a warm hug when he had told her about the notice. Joel had cried. He hurt inside but he felt better when his mum held him. The smell of her apron made him feel safe.

Joel had gone to bed early with a hot chocolate drink. In spite of being upset, he slept well. He was unaware of the doorbell ringing shortly after he went to bed. It was Andy's dad wanting to know if Joel was all right because he had been missed at training. Mr Green explained about Norman to Mr Jones. Ben hadn't cried when told the news but he had been very quiet for the rest of the evening.

On the way to school next morning, Joel still felt numb. He had a note from his mum for Mr Davies, his class teacher, explaining that he had received some bad news about the death of a friend.

Jimmy and Andy had decided not to cycle to school on that Tuesday morning. So all three sat together on the school bus. Jimmy and Andy were talking about both being in the team for the Makerley game.

"If you'd come to training, Joel, you could have been picked too. Then we'd all have been playing together," said Andy brightly.

"I was coming but I had to go home suddenly," Joel muttered.

"Why?" Andy was concerned and had realised that Joel was upset. Joel told them about finding the notice on Albert's door.

"Dead! So that was why he didn't come on Saturday," said Jimmy. He was beginning to sound like a detective again. "Did the notice say how he died? I mean, was it suspicious?"

"No, it didn't say," replied Joel sharply.

Jimmy and Andy resumed their conversation about the Makerley game. Joel gazed quietly out of the window. The sky was grey and cloudy. A few drops of rain were spotting on the bus windows. Joel thought about Norman. He missed him. He was sad not to be having any more talks in the back room of the shop. No more treats on a tray. No more warm smiles.

By lunchtime, word had got round among the crowd who had come to the bike test that Norman Albert had died and that Joel was upset. Not all the children were as kind and sensitive to Joel as Andy had been. Martin Harrison said that Dave Chapman stood no chance in the trials now Norman Albert was dead. Joel didn't know what to say.

One girl, Rosie Graham, asked loudly, "What happens when you die, then? Is that the end?"

A boy called Daniel Harvey replied, "My dad says that when we die our body just rots in the ground. He says we have to work hard and take all the chances we can to live a happy life now."

"Sounds a bit sad," said Rosie. Joel stood on the edge of a group of five children near the bike sheds. He listened in silence as the discussion went on.

An Indian boy called Suhil said, "We Hindus believe that we don't rot in the ground but our bodies are changed into something else and we come back again. It may be something better, like a king or worse like a snake. It depends how well we live this life."

"I wouldn't mind being the king but I don't think I fancy the snake much," laughed Rosie.

A boy called Ian Mitchell was waiting for a break in the conversation. He quietly added, "I believe when we die we go to be with Jesus, in heaven."

"That's what my grandma used to say when she was alive!" exclaimed Joel.

The bell sounded. Joel moved away towards the Year 6 entrance. So many different views. He wanted to believe them all but felt he couldn't. He liked the idea of heaven being a happy place. He smiled as he thought of Norman's joke about cycling in heaven. Joel remembered how Norman hadn't seemed afraid of death when Joel had talked to him outside the church. Some of his friends' ideas of dying made him feel scared but Norman's view made him feel warm and happy. Ian Mitchell seemed to believe the same as Norman about dying. Joel felt sure Norman was in heaven with God.

Dad came home at six thirty. He said "hello" to everyone and then sat down in the lounge to read the evening paper. After a couple of minutes he rustled the pages importantly, folded one of the sheets back and said, "Hey Joel. There's an article on your friend Norman in the paper." Dad cleared his throat and then read in a loud voice:

Death of Former Champion

Norman Albert, former national cycling champion, died of a heart attack at his home last Saturday morning. He was aged 68.

Mr Albert had run his own bike shop in Edensbury since his retirement from professional racing thirty years ago.

The funeral will be held at 2 pm on Friday 25 April at St Thomas' Church, Edensbury.

Mr Green passed the paper to Joel. Ben looked over Joel's shoulder. There were two pictures of Norman. One was a recent one and the other was the picture of him with the Milk Race trophy. It was just like the one on the wall in the shop. Joel asked to have the cutting for his scrapbook. Mr

Green agreed but told Joel he would have to wait until tomorrow to have the paper to cut up. Joel decided he would start a new section of his scrapbook for Norman Albert.

Later, Joel sat in the kitchen with his mum. She was rolling out some pastry on the kitchen table. Joel was making patterns with his finger in the flour.

"Mum? Do you think I could go to Norman's funeral?"

"On your own?"

"No. You and Dad could take me."

"I don't know. Dad would have to get time off work. Ben may want to come too. We need to think about it."

It happened that Dad was due a half day off from work that week and so could arrange to finish work on Friday lunchtime. He was free to go to the funeral. Both he and Mrs Green thought it important that they help Joel. Joel felt he wanted to go and say "Thank you" to God for Norman.

Joel lay on his bed that night, thinking about Dave. The trials were only two and a half weeks away. The bike had passed its first test at Osterton but how would it do in competition? Would Dave make it into the Olympic team? What if Martin Harrison was right? How would Dave manage without his friend Norman to make alterations and give advice? Joel wondered, too, whether Dave would be at the funeral on Friday.

Chapter fourteen

Saying goodbye

Today was the day of the funeral. Joel felt he wanted to go. He wasn't quite sure what to expect but he sensed it was an important occasion. Mum and Dad seemed to think so too. Dad had got his dark suit cleaned yesterday. He had been wearing a white shirt and black tie at breakfast this morning. It was different from the ties he usually wore to work. Joel and Ben were going to wear school uniform for the funeral.

It was nearly twenty to two when Mr Green turned the car into the church car park. A crowd was already gathering outside the covered gateway to the church. Three large black cars were parked close by. The first car didn't have any passenger seats at the back. Instead it had a flat raised bench that made it look like a very smart estate car. Dad said this car was called a hearse and was used for carrying the coffin.

As they entered the church, two men dressed in black suits showed them to their seats. Organ music was playing softly in the background. They were shuffling along the bench seats when a young man slipped into the row with them and sat next to Joel. He dug Joel in the ribs playfully and smiled at him. It was Dave. He was wearing a dark suit just like Mr Green. Ben and Joel smiled back and then Joel introduced Dave to his mum and dad. There wasn't much time to talk before the service began but Mr Green leaned across Joel towards Dave and whispered loudly, "Pleased to meet you Dave. Sorry to be meeting you on an occasion like this."

Dave smiled again. He seemed to put the Greens at ease with just a smile.

Joel could see the coffin on a stand at the front of the church. A bunch of flowers in the shape of a cycling helmet was arranged on the polished oak casket. As the service began everyone stood to sing the hymn "Abide with me". Joel had heard the song before when he had watched the FA Cup Final on TV. Dave was singing loudly next to him. Joel was glad Dave was there. It wouldn't have seemed right without him.

Everyone sat down at the end of the hymn. The vicar started talking about Norman. Joel felt a lump in his throat; he found it hard to swallow. Although he was sad that Norman was dead, he felt a happy glow inside as he thought about him. The vicar mentioned some things about Norman that Joel didn't know. He said how Norman had helped organise a camp every summer for the children from the Osterton children's home. He had done this for over twenty years, only finishing when he was sixty-five. He also said that Norman and his wife Jean had been very active in the church. They had helped run the children's work for fifteen years.

During the singing of the next hymn, Dave suddenly left Joel's side and walked to the front of the church. He stood behind a big book which was on a stand. Mr Green told Joel that it was the Bible.

Dave read out loud for everyone to hear, "The Lord is my shepherd, I shall lack nothing..." Joel especially remembered the words "though I walk through the valley of the shadow of death, I will not be afraid. For you are with me..." Maybe that was why Norman was unafraid of death – because God was with him. Joel felt that another piece of the jigsaw had fitted into place. He looked aside at his mum and dad. They were both gazing admiringly at Dave. Dave was reading clearly and strongly as if the words in the passage had special meaning for him. As he finished reading there was total silence. Dave's shoes clicked on the stone floor as he walked back to his seat.

Joel noticed a woman at the front of the church who was bent forward. Her shoulders were shaking gently. With one hand she dabbed a white handkerchief against her tear-stained cheek. With the other hand she fingered a white pearl necklace which hung round her neck. Joel felt there was something familiar about her. Where had he seen her before?

As the last hymn played, the coffin was carried out on the shoulders of six men. Two of the men were the ones who had shown the Greens to their seat. They were all dressed in the same black clothes. The congregation filed out behind the coffin which was carried to the churchyard.

As they followed, Joel could see the mound of freshly dug earth and the bright green strip around the hole. A straggly line of people crossed the graveyard behind the coffin. Joel and his mum stayed on the path, some distance from the grave-side, where they could see what was happening. Mr Green and Ben joined the group behind the coffin. Joel couldn't hear what was said as everyone gathered around the grave. He could tell the vicar was speaking. Lots of people had their heads bowed. The men carrying the coffin stood still with it on their shoulders.

After what seemed a long time the six men lowered the coffin into the hole. Then some earth was shovelled into the hole. After a few moments, people lifted their heads. Small groups of people moved slowly away from the grave-side. Some people were crying or hugging each other as the funeral came to an end.

Dave Chapman came over with Joel's dad and Ben and spoke to Joel's mum. "I'm sorry we didn't get much chance to talk," Dave said.

"No. Well, it wasn't the time, was it really? But

we are ever so pleased to meet you. Joel's told us so much about you. Hasn't he, Bill?"

"He has. Joel reckons you'll win a gold for Britain," Mr Green added.

"Well, I'll have to get into the team first. That's the big hurdle, but Norman has been brilliant in getting the bike ready in time. It's only a shame he won't be here to see me race."

The conversation was interrupted by the arrival of the tall elderly woman with the pearl necklace. She put out her hand towards Dave. Joel noticed her long thin fingers and the rings on them.

"Dave, how nice that you could come."

"I wanted to come, Jean. Norman was very special to me. You have both been so kind."

Jean? Joel had heard that name. Jean Albert. The rings on her fingers reminded him of Baines' on the day his bike was stolen. This was the same woman. Mrs Albert! Of course, it was Norman's wife.

Dave was introducing Mrs Albert to Mr and Mrs Green. Then it was Ben and Joel's turn. As she looked at Joel she stopped. Her mouth fell open and she let out a laugh. Several of the other mourners who were milling around outside the church appeared quite surprised to hear Mrs Albert laugh.

"Of course. The boy who lost his bike at Baines'! You're Joel Green. I should have realised."

"Realised what?" asked Joel shyly.

"That you were the boy that Norman talked about. He told me about your bike being stolen but

I never made the connection with us having met at Baines'. How stupid of me! You know, Norman talked so much about you. I know you only met recently but he really talked about you as a special friend."

Joel blushed and looked down. Mrs Albert continued, "Any friend of Norman's is a friend of mine."

"Thank you," said Joel.

"Look, Joel, Ben, Mr and Mrs Green. I really would be most pleased if you would all have tea with me one day. Not this week because there is so much to sort out now Norman has gone. What about a week tomorrow? Four o'clock? I live at 28 Somerton Road."

"Thank you, Mrs Albert," Joel's mum was saying, "but don't you think it's a bit soon after Norman's death? I mean, you might not feel up to it."

"Nonsense, my dear. I want you to come. I will be glad of the company." Mrs Albert turned to move away to a group of elderly ladies. Joel's dad called after her, "Thank you. We'll be there."

In the car on the way home, Joel began to wonder about going to visit Mrs Albert. He wasn't sure he would go. He had wanted to go to the funeral but that was all. He felt he wanted to forget mountain bikes and Norman and Dave for a while. Tomorrow was the Makerley game. Joel wished he were playing. He thought perhaps he would go and watch. The Colts could do with some support.

Chapter fifteen

Two surprises for Joel

Joel's support couldn't prevent Edensbury's defeat. It wasn't the only bad thing about that week. Joel felt tired and fed up most of the time. Digger couldn't understand why Joel got so cross when he accidentally slobbered on his shoes on Tuesday night. He thought his master would enjoy some affection. He didn't bargain for Joel kicking out at him. Mum sent Joel to his room to calm down. Joel was glad to get out of the way.

It was unusual for Joel to be told off by his mum. He lay on his bed sulking. He felt as if he wanted to cry but he bit his lip and tried to think about something else. He tried to keep his mind off mountain bikes but he couldn't.

The week edged slowly towards Saturday. Joel hadn't forgotten Mrs Albert's invitation. He wished his dad hadn't accepted it. As the day came nearer, it began to feel more like a visit to the dentist than a treat to look forward to.

On that dull, cloudy Saturday morning, Joel

took Digger for a long walk down by the river. It took Joel twenty minutes to catch Digger, who had been chasing rabbits.

As he bent down to put him on the lead, Joel noticed a bicycle wheel sticking out of the reeds by the edge of the river. He ran over to it. His heart was pounding as he pulled the wheel from the mud. Soon a tangled bike frame was next to him on the river bank. There was only one wheel, the pedals were broken and the saddle was missing. It was his BMX bike. Joel left it on the bank and ran home with Digger.

Mr Green phoned the police when Joel told him about the BMX. The police said they would collect the bike in case they needed it for evidence. Joel didn't want to see the bike any more and he didn't care who had taken it. He lay on his bed until it was time to leave for Mrs Albert's. Ben had offered Joel a go on his mountain bike, to cheer him up, but Joel hadn't been interested.

Later that afternoon the Greens were in Mrs Albert's large front room. Joel and Ben sat next to Mum on the sofa. Dad sat in a high-backed armchair in the corner of the room by a glass-fronted trophy cabinet. Mrs Albert smiled, "Now I expect you're hungry, Joel."

Joel nodded politely.

She left the room in the direction of the kitchen. Joel and his brother looked at the trophies in the cabinet. The ornamental clock on the mantlepiece ticked loudly. In the background Joel could hear the clattering of china teacups and saucers. When Mrs Albert appeared round the door a few moments later, with a large tray. Joel stared at it closely. There was lots of food on it – sandwiches, pork pies, sausage rolls and two different sorts of crisps. Mrs Albert set the tray down on the coffee table in the centre of the lounge. Then she went back out to the kitchen quickly to fetch the drinks.

When Mrs Albert finally sat down, Joel had been given a plate piled high with food and a glass of orangeade to enjoy. There was also a large chocolate cake to look forward to. It was just like the one that Norman had shared with Joel in the shop. Joel kicked his feet happily as he munched his peanut butter sandwiches. This was turning out much better than he hoped.

"Mrs Albert, Norman must have worked very hard to get Dave's bike finished in time for the Olympic trials," said Joel's mum.

"He really did," Mrs Albert replied. "So many things went wrong whilst he was trying to finish it. The delay of the gear part from Italy was only one of several problems he had with the bike. With each set-back Norman got more tired and strained. Dave was very good and didn't force Norman to go any faster than he could but Norman didn't want to let Dave down. He wanted to give Dave the best possible chance of a place in the team. It seemed Norman just tried too hard. The strain probably brought on his heart attack."

Mrs Green leant forward in her chair and spoke softly to Mrs Albert. "You must miss Norman so much."

Mrs Albert put her tea cup down.

"I do. I really do." Her eyes filled with tears. "But it is good to know that he is with God. I am happy that we will meet again one day." She smiled at the thought.

Joel hoped Norman would be rewarded by Dave winning a place in the Olympic team. The trials were next Saturday at Makerley Forest. Joel thought that as this was virtually home territory for Dave, he should do well.

Mrs Albert gathered up the tea things and took them to the kitchen. Joel smiled, he had enjoyed his tea. When Mrs Albert returned, she had a sparkle in her eye and a smile on her face. "Well," she said importantly, "I hope you won't mind but I have a surprise for Joel."

Joel's mouth dropped open. His eyes were wide with excitement. Mrs Albert continued, "No. Actually there are two surprises. Come with me into the back room."

Mr and Mrs Green stood up hesitantly but Joel leapt from his seat and rushed after Mrs Albert. Ben followed more slowly.

As they entered the tidy dining-room, Joel looked around eagerly. There was a long, shiny, dark wooden table in the centre of the room which had six chairs around it. At the far end of the room was a writing desk. Leaning up against it was a brand new red and black mountain bike.

"Here is your surprise, Joel. Norman wanted you to have it, but he wasn't able to give it to you before he died. It's one he made himself." Mrs Albert was beaming as she spoke.

"Wow!" Ben gasped.

Joel was jumping up and down. "Oh, thank you! Can I ride it now?"

Joel's dad answered, "You can ride it home if you like, son." He turned to Mrs Albert, "This is amazing. Are you sure it's all right for him to have this?"

"Oh, goodness me, yes." Mrs Albert sounded a bit like she did when she had spoken to Mr Graham at Baines'. Joel wheeled the shiny bike round the table. Ben eyed it closely. He was genuinely pleased for his younger brother. Now they could go mountain biking together.

"Oh wait! I said two surprises, didn't I?" Mrs Albert pulled a long white envelope off the top of the writing desk. She handed it to Joel. He ripped the envelope open. Inside was a letter. As Joel unfolded the letter, some tickets dropped on the floor. Mrs Green picked them up. Joel read out loud:

"Dear Joel,

Hope you like Norman's surprise for you. I have a surprise too. Here are some passes for you and your family to come to the Olympic trial on Saturday 10 May at Makerley Forest as my special guests. Look forward to seeing you then.

Best wishes

    Dave Chapman

P S There are passes for Jimmy and Andy too."

Joel looked at the passes, then at his new bike, then at Mrs Albert and his mum and dad. To think he hadn't wanted to come! Later that evening, Ben let Joel try on his new black cycle helmet for size.

"The colour goes great with your mountain bike." Ben said encouragingly. "Perhaps you could get one as well. I've still got the advert." Joel didn't reply as his dad called him away to the phone.

It was Dave. "Hi, Joel. I've just spoken to Jean Albert. I gather you like the bike."

"Oh, yes! It's a hand–built one just like yours. Well, not as fast, but you know what I mean. Oh, thanks for the passes to the trials. We're really looking forward to coming."

"No problem. I want you to be there. Was Jean all right this afternoon?"

"Yeah, she was a bit sad when Mum talked to her about Norman but she became happier when she talked about him being with Jesus."

"Norman's in a good place, now," said Dave. "He lived his life God's way and now he has his reward. You know, we only get one crack at life, Joel, and Norman chose to live to please Jesus."

"Yes, he once told me that we each have to choose which route to take in life," said Joel, thinking of his conversation with Norman outside St Thomas'. "What did he mean, Dave?"

Dave paused before answering. "Think about it like this. A few weeks ago, you didn't know me. You might have read about me in one of those magazines Ben reads, but we had never met. You didn't know me personally. Now we've met and we are getting to know each other. We can choose to get to know each other even better. It's the same with Jesus. We need to be introduced to him and then we need to choose to get to know him better. I think that's what Norman meant."

Joel was quiet for a moment, then he said, "I see."

Dave continued, "Norman introduced you to me and helped us to get to know each other. I'm really glad he did. In the same way, I can help you to know Jesus, Joel, if you would like."

Joel felt sure he would like that.

"I'm really glad we can be friends," said Dave. "Perhaps we can talk some more, once I've got the trials over. Anyway, I'll look out for you all next Saturday."

"Thanks, Dave. Bye."

Now he had a new bike and a special pass to the Olympic Mountain Bike Trials, Joel couldn't wait for next Saturday.

Chapter sixteen

A special thank you

"Hey Joel! Have you heard about Martin Harrison?" Jimmy ran up to Joel excitedly in the playground. "He's been suspended from school! He was with some Year 9 boys who took some boxes of cigarettes from a delivery van at the back of Baines'. They were caught selling them at school."

"Really?" gasped Joel.

"Yeah. Pity we couldn't have caught them. We might have got a reward."

"Well, what about the bike you saw Harrison selling?" Joel asked.

Jimmy looked down at his feet. "We found out from his younger brother that it was his old mountain bike. Neil used it for a few months then they sold it. Sorry we couldn't find out who took your bike, Joel."

"Not to worry," smiled Joel. "I've got my own Norman Albert special now!" Joel then told Jimmy what had happened the previous Saturday: how sad he had been to find his own bike and the wonderful surprises from Jean Albert and Dave Chapman.

That Monday whilst Joel was at school, Mr Green got Joel's new bike security-coded. Every spare moment of the following week, Joel was riding it. Jimmy and Andy were delighted now Joel had his own bike again. The three friends and Ben had their own mountain bike trial in Osterton Country Park on Friday night, the day before Dave's trial at Makerley.

Joel didn't sleep well on the night before the Olympic trial. He was too excited. He dreamt that he and Dave Chapman were racing their mountain bikes near the end of the Olympic trial. As they fought shoulder to shoulder, their wheels became locked. The finish line was in sight. Suddenly they both fell off. Joel woke up as the trophy was presented to Martin Harrison who had come from nowhere to win. Joel sat up in bed, wiping the sleep from his eyes. He was glad it was only a dream.

Joel felt worried for Dave. He hoped Dave would make the Olympic team. What if the bike broke? Joel leant across and switched on the bedside light. Four o'clock. In a few hours they would know if Dave was in the team. Joel turned off the light. Ben was still fast asleep. Joel tried to settle down but he didn't sleep well at all.

At last, the family were on their way. As they neared the forest, police patrolmen in fluorescent yellow jackets and motorcycle boots marshalled the traffic. Special road signs appeared at various intervals, giving directions to the forest. The Greens joined long queues of cars going to the trials. Joel was bouncing up and down on the back seat in excitement. Mr Green had to tell him to stop several times.

The passes they had been given allowed them into a fenced-off area where a temporary grandstand had been put up. This was right by the start/finish line. Mr Green showed the passes to a woman steward. She handed them a glossy booklet which gave the order of the races. She pointed out their seats. Jimmy and Andy were already waiting in the seats next to the ones reserved for the Greens.

"Hey, Joel! What about this? Our own seats in the stands!" shouted Jimmy as they approached.

"Do you think people know Dave Chapman gave us these seats?" Andy asked in an equally loud voice.

"They probably do now," muttered Mr Green under his breath.

The programme showed that the trials took the form of three heats. The first three finishers in each heat were to go through to the final. The first two riders to finish in the final would be awarded the places in the Olympic team. Dave was in the second heat.

The riders had to do four laps of the course. So the spectators in the grandstand got to see the racers five times including the start. Dave did well in his heat, finishing second. By the time all the heats had been run, Dave was fifth fastest of all the riders in the final. Joel was puzzled. He knew Dave was good enough to make the team. Why wasn't he faster?

The nine men lined up for the final. Dave had got drawn on the outside, which was not the best place to start from. Riders on the inside usually did better. Dave looked up to the stand from the starting line. He caught sight of Joel and Ben and gave a thumbs up sign. Joel smiled and waved back.

"Come on, Dave," he shouted. Andy and Jimmy joined in shouting too.

Dave was up against Dean Rankin, the former British champion. Dave would need to be at his best to beat him. The starting pistol fired and the riders sped off into the forest. The roar of the crowd died down until the riders reappeared a few minutes later at the end of the first lap. Dean Rankin had a five second lead over the second place rider. Dave Chapman was third. The places remained unchanged at the end of the second lap but Dean's lead was now eight seconds.

Some of the riders were tiring and the field was stretching out. As the riders came into view at the end of the third lap, Dave was in second place. Dean Rankin was only four seconds ahead. If it stayed like this Dave would qualify for the team but Joel knew Dave wanted to win the race.

A huge roar greeted the riders as they started

the final lap. Joel and his friends were standing up in excitement. They craned their necks in the direction from which the riders would approach the line. The forest track was quiet. A hush descended on the crowd. Mr Green stood up and looked down the finishing straight. Then he saw Dave's purple helmet in the lead as he was hunched over the handlebars. He was powering for home. Dean Rankin was right on Dave's shoulder.

Mrs Green's shrill voice rose above the others, "Come on Dave! You can do it!"

Mr Green looked sideways at his wife in surprise. From where they were in the stand, Joel saw Dave's purple helmet edge in front and shoot past them to cross the line in first place. Dave had won the Olympic trial! He was in the team! Norman's bike had done it. It was a new British record too, easily within the Olympic qualifying time.

The next few minutes were chaos. A large section of the crowd rushed from the stand and mobbed Dave and Dean, the two qualifiers for the team. Camera bulbs flashed and several reporters shouted questions across the crowd to Dave. As the scrum of people edged back in front of the stand, a podium was put out ready for the presentation. A microphone was hastily put in front of the platform. The crowd began to return to their seats. One of the organisers stood up at the mike.

"Ladies and gentlemen. There will now be a

presentation of medals to the two qualifiers for the Olympic team."

Dean Rankin was given his medal first. There was a pause before Dave Chapman was called to the rostrum to receive his medal. The Greens, Jimmy and Andy stood and cheered when Dave was called forward. Joel thought his heart would burst, he was so happy for Dave. Dave smiled broadly and waved to the crowd. There were more photographs to pose for, this time with his medal. Then Dave moved forward to the microphone and a hush descended on the crowd.

"Ladies and gentlemen. I hardly know what to say. This is a dream come true. I always wanted to go to the Olympics to represent my country, and now I can." The crowd cheered again. Dave waited for silence then continued.

"Mountain biking is a great sport. I owe it a lot. But it's not the most important thing to me. I want to say thank you to some people who are more important than biking or medals. Firstly to God, for giving me health and a love of this sport. He is the reason I can do this sport well.

"Secondly, to Pete the Mechanic, for keeping me going this past winter when training was so hard. Thanks, Pete.

"Finally, thanks to a man called Norman Albert. He built my bike. Sadly he is not here today. He died a few weeks ago. He and his wife Jean are very special to me. When my own parents died in a car crash three years ago, Jean and Norman helped me through a very difficult time. I hope I can help Jean and also Norman's special friend, Joel Green, get through this sad experience." Joel blushed at the mention of his name.

"I hope that I can help by bringing back a medal from the Olympic games. It will be my way of saying a special thank you to Norman Albert – the Bicycle Man."

LET'S GO DISCOVERY

Another excellent **Let's Go** book!

If you enjoy puzzles, then you'll love the **Puzzle Zone**. Let Tara, Jack, Boff and all the other **Let's Go** characters lead you into a world of puzzles...

There are word-searches, picture mazes, spot-the-difference puzzles and quizzes. Each puzzle is based on Bible characters and passages, so you learn about the Bible and have fun at the same time. Time won't stand still!

ISBN 1 85999 186 6
Price £2.50
To buy your copy, visit your local Christian bookshop, or contact SU Direct on 01865 716880.